Angelina Ice Skates

To happy childhood memories of ice skating with my father, John Holabird   KH

To my great-niece, Emily, with love   HC

PUFFIN BOOKS

Published by the Penguin Group
Penguin Books Ltd, 80 Strand, London WC2R 0RL, England
Penguin Group (USA), Inc., 375 Hudson Street, New York, New York 10014, USA
Penguin Books Australia Ltd, 250 Camberwell Road, Camberwell, Victoria 3124, Australia
Penguin Books Canada Ltd, 10 Alcorn Avenue, Toronto, Ontario, Canada M4V 3B2
Penguin Ireland, 25 St Stephen's Green, Dublin 2, Ireland (a division of Penguin Books Ltd)
Penguin Books India (P) Ltd, 11 Community Centre, Panchsheel Park, New Delhi – 110 017, India
Penguin Group (NZ), cnr Airborne and Rosedale Roads, Albany, Auckland 1310, New Zealand
Penguin Books (South Africa) (Pty) Ltd, 24 Sturdee Avenue, Rosebank 2196, South Africa

Penguin Books Ltd, Registered Offices: 80 Strand, London WC2R 0RL, England

www.penguin.com

First published by ABC, All Books for Children, a division of The All Children's Company Ltd, 1993
Published by Viking 2001
1 3 5 7 9 10 8 6 4 2
Published in Puffin Books 2001
10

Printed in Italy by Printer Trento Srl

British Library Cataloguing in Publication Data
A CIP catalogue record for this book is available from the British Library

ISBN 0–670–91161–5 Hardback
ISBN 0–140–56869–7 Paperback

To find out more about Angelina, visit her web site at **www.angelinaballerina.com**

Angelina Ice Skates

Story by **Katharine Holabird** Illustrations by **Helen Craig**

PUFFIN BOOKS

Angelina absolutely loved snowy winter days when she could ice skate with her friends on Miller's Pond. The ice sparkled like glass and they raced across it in pairs, practising spins and twirls and figure-eights.

Everyone in the village was getting ready for New Year's Eve, and Angelina was preparing a special ice skating show. Her little cousin Henry wanted to be in the show, too, even though he often tumbled off the ice and fell into the snowbanks.

"We'll need someone to be the Snow King," said Angelina's friend Flora, pirouetting across the ice as the Snow Princess.

"I'll be the King!" shouted Henry, but then he tripped and slid into Alice, who was going to be the Snow Fairy.

"You'd be a better snow shovel!" said Alice crossly as she dusted off her skates.

"Don't worry, Henry," said Angelina. "Hold on to me and let's practise skating together."

They linked their tails and tried to skate in a circle, but it wasn't easy on the slippery ice. Just then Spike and Sammy, two big boys from school, raced by playing hockey and almost knocked them all over.

"HEY!" shouted Felicity, but the boys were already gone, laughing and yelling across the ice.

"Never mind," said Angelina, helping Felicity get her balance. "Let me show you how to skate backwards."

But, before long, Spike and Sammy tore past again, spraying snow in all directions. When they zipped through Angelina's rehearsal a third time, she got angry.

"Please stop interrupting us!" she scolded.

But the boys just laughed, grabbed Angelina's scarf, and tweaked Flora's whiskers.

"Little ballerinas can't catch us!" they shouted as they zoomed away.

Angelina and her friends chased Spike and Sammy all across the ice, and then Angelina made a huge snowball and hurled it at the boys.

"Great! A snowball fight!" Spike yelled, throwing one back at Angelina. Then everybody started throwing snowballs everywhere, and soon Miller's Pond was a blizzard of flying snow and shouting skaters.

They had so much fun, they stayed until Flora got ice down her neck and Alice's toes began to freeze. Then they trudged back to Angelina's house, feeling tired and frozen.

"What's wrong?" asked Angelina's mother.

"Our New Year's Eve Ice Dance is a mess," said Angelina sadly. "We haven't got costumes or scenery and Spike and Sammy keep bothering us."

"I can help you with costumes," said Mrs Mouseling. "And maybe the boys are teasing you because they want you to pay attention to them."

Angelina was surprised. "That gives me an idea."

The next day Angelina put on her skates and whizzed past Spike and Sammy, snatched their caps, and raced off laughing with the boys just behind her. They were very fast, but Angelina could do all sorts of tricky twists and spins and, just as Spike and Sammy thought they would grab her, she spun out of reach and they smashed into each other, collapsing on the ice.

Spike gazed at Angelina in admiration.
"You ballerinas are fast!"

"Would you like to be in our show?"
asked Angelina, tossing back their caps.

Spike and Sammy leaped up. "Yes!"
they shouted, skating in circles around her.

Sammy loved doing funny tricks and Spike, who could skate backwards, was proud to be the Snow King. Best of all, they helped Henry build a huge snow fort. "It will make a nice Snow Palace for our show," said Henry enthusiastically.

"What a great idea!" admired Angelina.

On New Year's Eve, the whole village dressed up and
came to celebrate. Miller's Pond looked magical as the

performers skated on to the ice in Mrs Mouseling's costumes,
and Henry's snow fort gleamed in the moonlight.

When Angelina danced into the spotlight that night, she felt just like a real snow queen. Spike and Sammy did exciting leaps and jumps together and Henry was thrilled to be the King's attendant, while Felicity, Flora, and Alice seemed to fly across the ice like delicate snowflakes.

At the end of the performance, as the magic hour
of midnight approached and fireworks sparkled in
the sky, Angelina and her friends wished everyone
joy and peace, and they all sang and danced
together to welcome in the New Year.